GHOST STORIES OF OLD TEXAS, II

GHOST STORIES OF OLD TEXAS, II

By

Zinita Fowler

Illustrated by

Jack Fowler

EAKIN PRESS ⬧ Fort Worth, Texas
www.EakinPress.com

Copyright © 1992
By Zinita Fowler
Published By Eakin Press
An Imprint of Wild Horse Media Group
P.O. Box 331779
Fort Worth, Texas 76163
1-817-344-7036
www.EakinPress.com
ALL RIGHTS RESERVED
1 2 3 4 5 6 7 8 9
Paperback ISBN 978-1-68179-247-7
eBook ISBN 978-1-68179-322-1

Library of Congress Cataloging-in-Publication Data

Fowler, Zinita.
    Ghost stories of Old Texas, II / by Zinita Fowler ; illustrated by Jack Fowler.
        p.   cm.
    Summary: A collection of ghostly tales illustrating the cultural heritage of Texas.
    ISBN 9781681792477
    1. Ghosts — Texas. 2. Tales — Texas. [1. Ghosts — Folklore.
    2. Folklore — Texas.] I. Fowler, Jack, ill. II. Title.
PZ8.1.F818Gh   1992
398.25 — dc20   92-19263
                                                             CIP
                                                              AC

This book is dedicated to my granddaughter
KARI,
who loves a good story.

Contents

Contents

Preface

In 1983, when I started telling the stories from *Ghost Stories of Old Texas,* I seldom finished a presentation without hearing from a student or teacher or someone else present, "Have you heard the one about — ?" After a time, I had collected enough of these I hadn't heard before to form the core of another book, and began writing them down. The result is this book.

For a story to be considered as a part of the collection, it must pass three tests:

Is it a genuine folktale, a true part of our Texas heritage?

Is it free of anything satanic or destructive to the minds of children?

Is it "tellable"? Does it make a good yarn for a storyteller to spin before an audience?

The stories herein passed all three tests. Read, enjoy, and go out to tell them yourself. That's what folklore is all about.

Bailey's Prairie

Down in southeast Texas in Brazoria County, there is a restless light that wanders about, appearing suddenly by day or night and disappearing just as quickly. It is most often seen on rainy nights when the wind is high. Big as a basketball, it bounces up and down and travels quickly across the flat terrain. Dogs for miles around turn their muzzles skyward and howl mournfully. Horses stomp restlessly in their stalls and whinny in fear.

People who live in the area say the light is the ghost of one Briton Bayle, or Brit Bailey. The spellings of the name may be different, but there is no mistaking the man.

Brit came to Texas even before Stephen F. Austin brought his colonists in the 1820s. He found some land he liked and squatted there, building a cabin and putting in some livestock. He was an eccentric man who liked to drink and fight. And he was very good with a gun.

It is said that Austin once went to Brit's cabin and told him he had no right to the land and had to

1

get out, right away. Austin found himself staring down the barrel of a shotgun, and backed away. Brit stayed. As far as he was concerned, the land was his and he meant to live there until he died. And that's exactly what he did.

Brit had some unusual ideas about his death. He left a will with instructions to bury him standing up and facing west, with his rifle on his shoulder and a jug of whiskey at his feet.

"I've never looked up to any man yet," Brit said. "And once I'm dead, I want no one to be able to say, 'Here lies Brit Bailey.'"

His wife, a pious woman, followed all but one of Brit's instructions after he died. She couldn't bring herself to put a jug of "devil's brew" in the coffin with her husband. She was certain he'd never get into heaven if she did.

The light, it is said, is old Brit looking for his jug of whiskey. It has come to be called Bailey's Light. And the land the old squatter loved and claimed to be his bears his name at last — Bailey's Prairie.

The Revenge of the Redhead

In the late 1800s, rich ore was discovered in the red soil near Rusk in East Texas. Speculators were quick to rush in, eager to get rich. Soon the piney woods were pushed back to make room for a boom town optimistically named New Birmingham.

As the mining business began to pay off, the town grew into a respectable place to live, with a sturdy red brick business district, churches, schools, and a newspaper — all well-lit by a system of electric lights.

The pride of the town was the four-story Southern Hotel, said to be one of the most luxurious in the South. It was built at a cost of $160,000, a staggering amount in those days, and was the center of the town's lively social life.

By 1880, the Tassie Belle furnace was turning out fifty tons of pig iron a day, and New Birmingham acquired the nickname "Iron Queen of the Southwest," or sometimes simply "Queen City." The sky seemed to be the limit, and hopes were high.

One of the early developers was a man known as

"the General." He lived with his beautiful red-haired wife in one of the suites of the hotel. As one of the founding fathers of the town, he was quite important in civic affairs. His wife was the leader of affluent society circles, and she loved being wined and dined and admired. She entertained the rich and famous, among them a U.S. president and many English lords.

New people were constantly moving into the booming town, hoping to make a fortune in the iron business. One such couple was a wealthy land developer from Tennessee and his dark-haired, buxom wife. His wife was a real beauty who could attract attention by merely walking into a room. Before long, she was challenging the General's wife as the queen of New Birmingham society.

Jealous of her position, the red-haired beauty was furious. She began to whisper stories that her rival was nothing more than a dance-hall girl whose husband had brought her to Texas to escape a sordid past. The gossip spread like wildfire, and soon the Tennessee beauty's reputation was ruined. She was ashamed to show her face in public.

Her husband was determined to find the source of the dreadful lies. Before long, he traced them to the General's wife. According to the custom of the day, he challenged the General to a duel, and shot him through the heart in the lobby of the Southern Hotel. He was arrested and tried, but a jury set him free. He left the state with his wife that very day.

The General's red-haired widow seemed to lose

her senses when the verdict was read. Screaming that the citizens were releasing a cold-blooded murderer who should be hanged, she ran through the streets of New Birmingham and called down curses from heaven on the town.

At first, the townspeople felt sorry for the poor, heartbroken woman. They tried to ignore her cries for revenge. She would soon come around and accept what had happened, they thought.

And then, a few weeks later, the Tassie Belle smelter blew up, for no apparent reason. Not long afterward, the town went dark when the electric plant burned to the ground. To add to the misfortunes, Governor Jim Hogg signed the Texas Alien Land Act. Because of this act, much of the money for developing the iron company which had been coming from wealthy overseas investors was now against the law.

The mine soon closed down, and people began to move away. Houses and buildings were deserted and began to decay as the forest moved back in to reclaim the land. By the beginning of the twentieth century, the "Iron Queen of the Southwest" was a ghost town.

Historians give logical reasons for the town's demise. But a few old-timers who know the legend of what happened merely shake their heads and smile. They know that New Birmingham was doomed from the moment the General's red-haired widow called down a curse on it from the sky.

Le Loup Blanc

The early Cajun settlers on the Bolivar Peninsula near Galveston were often awakened on foggy nights by eerie howls coming from somewhere in the darkness. Fearing it might be some kind of evil spirit, they cowered in their beds and would not go outside to investigate.

Soon, however, they began to discover on the mornings after the howlings that some of their chickens were missing. They decided that perhaps the howls were coming from a more earthly animal. The next time the howling was heard, some of the best hunting dogs were sent out to chase away whatever it might be. They returned in bad shape, clawed and beaten, and nothing could make them go out into the darkness again. Every time they heard the howls after that, the dogs would slink under the house and refuse to come out until morning.

Finally, when they continued to lose their poultry, some of the braver men decided to hide in the barn to see what the thing might be. What they saw sent chills up their spines.

Out of the fog came a figure about the size of a small horse, but in the shape of a wolf. It was shimmering white, almost blending with the gray mist that rose from the ground. When it sat back on its haunches, pointed its nose skyward, and gave the mournful howl that was now familiar to the settlers, one of the men put his gun to his shoulder and fired.

At once, the wolf turned and loped away toward the swamp. The men followed, firing into the fog. At the edge of the *prarie tremblant,* the Cajun name for the treacherous marshes that hold sinkholes and quicksand, the wolf disappeared. Any man who tried to follow him would be risking his life.

The settlers named the ghostly animal Le Loup Blanc, which means The White Wolf. He appeared several times after that, but always led his pursuers to the dangerous marshes. There he disappeared, some say into thin air. As time went by, sightings of the wolf were made further apart, and his eerie howls were seldom heard.

Could he still be there, lurking in the marshes? Will he appear again some foggy night to send his mournful howl through the mist to make the farmers snuggle deeper under their covers and the dogs creep to safety under the house?

It could happen, say the believers.

A Town of Ghosts

Jefferson, in far East Texas, is a town in which many historic things have happened. When Texas was a republic, Jefferson was a busy riverport and a center of industry. During the Civil War, many rich merchants and manufacturers built mansions there that were designed and furnished as elegantly as any in the country. A fine hotel, the Excelsior, was in the center of town and furnished lodging and entertainment for presidents, millionaires, and other famous people who came through the town.

Toward the end of the century, however, the fortunes of the town had turned. Its days of grandeur were over. One reason was that a dam holding back water from the Big Cypress Bayou was destroyed. This ruined the riverboat traffic and brought an end to the shipping industry in Jefferson. Another was that Jay Gould, a millionaire railroader who wanted to make his headquarters in the town, grew angry with the city fathers. He declared he would see to it that Jefferson became a ghost town.

Had it not been for the Excelsior Hotel, Gould's

8

curse against the town might have worked. With businesses failing and people moving away, the fine old hostelry continued to offer shelter, fine food, and good service to travelers passing through.

Today Jefferson is but a shadow of the former bustling place it used to be. But it has transformed into one of the biggest tourist attractions in the state. Reservations at the Excelsior have to be made months in advance. And among the many interesting places to visit is Jay Gould's lavishly furnished Pullman car, in which he traveled from place to place.

And so, Jefferson did not become a ghost town, like many of the ports along the Brazos River. It has, however, become a town of ghosts, one of which is said to live inside the Excelsior Hotel. This spirit has been sighted in many forms by persons from various walks of life. Sometimes it has shape and form; other times it only makes strange noises, breathes loudly, and whips the window curtains about. A room that was a favorite of Jay Gould seems to be the one in which the ghost is most often sighted. Perhaps it is the spirit of the crusty old financier, still angry at the town and unable to rest.

Ghostly forms and "cold spots" have also appeared in several of the historic old mansions which have been restored to their former grandeur. Many ruins of buildings in old downtown Jefferson are said to be inhabited by unworldly creatures. So are the rotting wharfs down by the Bayou.

Old-timers who have lived in the area all their lives seem to take the spirits as a matter of course. They will speak to you of their own sightings totally without fear.

The Lady in Black

Don Ramos was a handsome young Spanish rancher. He was also rich, owning great herds of cattle which roamed over the flat coastal plains northwest of where the city of Corpus Christi now stands. When he built a fine *hacienda*, the eligible girls from nearby ranches had hopes that he was ready to marry and settle down. One in particular had yearned after Don Ramos for some time. She now waited expectantly for him to call on her father and ask for her hand.

She waited in vain. When Don Ramos returned from a trip to Mexico, he brought with him a beautiful bride named Leonora. They settled into the lovely ranch house and were happy.

They had been married for only a few months when business matters called Don Ramos away to Spain. In the 1700s, that was a long and dangerous trip. Sadly, he took leave of his young wife, knowing she would be safe in the care of her devoted *duena*.

Don Ramos was gone for many months. When he returned, Leonora told him joyfully that they were going to have a child. He was delighted, and for a few days, the reunion with his wife was a time of great joy. His happiness soon turned to dismay and then to dark fury when rumors reached his ears that Leonora had been unfaithful while he was away. The child was not his, they said. The rumors were supposedly started by the disappointed girl who had wanted to be his wife.

Leonora wept and begged him to believe that she loved only him and would never be untrue. Her pleas fell on deaf ears. Don Ramos' pride was devastated.

"Dress her in black," he ordered the sobbing *duena*. Then he stormed out to the quarters of his *vaqueros*. "You will escort Dona Leonora one day northward," he told them. "At dusk, find a tall tree and hang her!"

Perhaps the cowboys were horrified and perhaps not. In those days, a man was the king of his household, and his orders were obeyed without question. Further, they had never seen their *padron* so angry.

Once Leonora realized she was doomed, it was as though she turned to ice. "I am innocent," she told the riders. "I will never let any of you forget this thing you do."

She has kept her vow. On the lonely roads around Alice, Ben Bolt, and Falfurrias, persons have told of seeing a tall, slender figure in black by the side of the road. Those who stop to see if the lady needs help find no one there. Since there are no trees

12

or underbrush in many spots where the lady has been seen, the claim is made that she simply disappears.

Old-timers from this area have been told Leonora's sad story since they were children. They know who the Lady in Black beside the road is. It is the spirit of a broken-hearted young wife keeping her promise: "I will never let you forget."

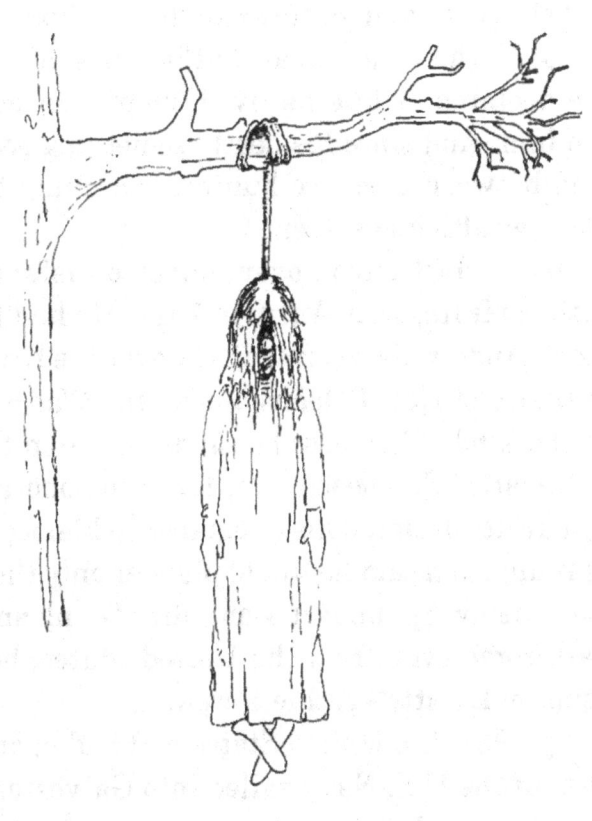

Hidden Pirate Treasure

"No greedy adventurer shall ever have any of my gold!" the pirate Jean LaFitte is said to have once declared. While he lived, no one dared steal from him. And since his death, something seems to stand between treasure-hunters searching for the hidden wealth and success.

Jean LaFitte took over Galveston Island from another pirate, Luis Aury, in 1817. He had been a hero in Andrew Jackson's victory over the British at the Battle of New Orleans during the War of 1812. But the kind of business he carried on from the colony he called Campeachy was far from honorable.

LaFitte declared his allegiance to Mexico in the beginning, and said he would plunder only the ships of the enemy, Spain. But soon, ships flying any flag at all, some even from the United States, became victims of LaFitte's ruthless crew.

By 1821, the United States had had enough. A vessel of the U.S. Navy sailed into Galveston with orders that LaFitte must leave at once. Quickly, the pirate chief and his men took the treasure they had

not already hidden and loaded it onto LaFitte's flagship, *The Pride*. Then they raced out to the open sea.

No one knows their fate. Some say they headed for the Caribbean and were lost in a storm at sea. Coast-dwelling Indians declared that the schooner was sunk under fire in a lonely bayou near Sabine Pass and all hands were lost. They further claim to have seen a ghostly figure in pirate garb lurking near the spot where the ship went down.

Many stories are told of treasure-hunters with maps to various spots where LaFitte's treasure is to be found. One man returned in such a state of terror from his expedition that he couldn't tell anyone what happened. He died within a few days. Others say the horror they experienced was too terrible to recall, and they warn others to stay away.

Much of the loot was supposed to have been buried on Galveston Island. An old Spaniard appeared one day at a farmhouse near the Brazos River. His face was horribly scarred; he was also emaciated and burning with fever. The farmer took him in, and for several days the man hovered near death. Then he began to recover.

"You have been kind to me," he told the farmer. "And so, I will share my secret with you."

He said that he had been one of LaFitte's men on Galveston Island. He was on the other side of the island, guarding a treasure, when LaFitte was ordered to leave. Thus he was left behind. When he realized what had happened, he buried the treasure chests, one filled with silver and one with gold. Then he ran for his life, and stayed hidden for many years. Now that LaFitte was dead and interest in the pirate had waned, the old man was going back to Galveston to get the treasure.

"Only I know where it is," he said, his dark eyes glittering. "And if you will help me, I will share it with you. We will both be rich — very rich!"

The farmer was tempted. Work was hard on his small farm, and money in short supply. Still, he knew nothing of this Spaniard, except that he might have been a pirate. The farmer didn't know what to do. Finally, after talking it over with his wife, he agreed to go with the man.

"Be wary, dear husband," the wife said. "If he

seems to threaten you in any way, run away and come back home."

At first, the trip seemed like an adventure to the farmer. But the Spaniard was old and still weak from his illness, and their pace was slow. By the second night, the farmer was beginning to have doubts. This man might be capable of doing anything to get all the gold for himself.

At the close of the second day, they made camp and settled down for the night. Suddenly, night seemed to turn to day. The sky was filled with brilliant balls of fire that shot off in every direction to explode in bursts of white light. Certain it was a sign to warn him away from the old Spaniard, the farmer saddled his horse and galloped away toward home, leaving the old man behind.

When he arrived at home, he cried out to his wife, "The old man is some kind of devil! I was warned away from him by great bursts of fire in the sky."

The woman quickly reassured him. "No, my dear. It was simply a night of many falling stars. We saw it here as well."

A few days later, a traveler on horseback stopped by the farmhouse. He had a packet to deliver. It was from the old Spaniard.

"I found him at a campsite, very ill," the man explained. "Before he died, he asked me to deliver this to you."

It was a map of Galveston Island with an X

marking the spot where the treasure chests were hidden.

The farmer wanted nothing more to do with it. "It is wrong to want riches that were stolen from others," he said. "Look what has happened to the old man. And perhaps if I had not heeded the warning that was sent to me, who knows what my fate may have been." He told his wife to put the map away, and she hid it in a cupboard.

Sometime later, the farmer was telling a friend about the old Spaniard and the pirate treasure. When he opened the cupboard to show him the map, it was gone. No one had been in the house who might have stolen it. It had simply disappeared.

And so, LaFitte and his crew of cutthroats are said to roam the Texas coastline, forever protecting their treasure from anyone who wants to claim it.

The Face on the Wall

Ewing Hall at the University of Texas Medical Branch in Galveston was built as a simple, solid gray building. Several years after it became a part of the school, a strange image appeared on one of the panels that faces the bay. A pattern of light and dark, about ten by seven feet, formed the features of a bearded man, his eyes staring intently out to sea.

Texas history buffs declare that the face is a likeness of Jean LaFitte, the notorious pirate who made his headquarters in Galveston back in the 1800s. It seems logical to them that since the pirate is said to have buried much of his treasure on the island, he would want to stand guard over it. Apparently, he is doing a good job. To this day, no one has located any appreciable amount of his loot.

More realistic folk declare that the pattern is only made up of shadows or perhaps moisture in the concrete, and there is really no face there at all. Others say they see it, but they aren't sure if it is LaFitte.

The building is there. Next time you visit Galveston, drop by it and decide for yourself.

The Lost Musicians

El ninja is a dark cloud of dust that appears suddenly and sweeps back and forth across the Texas Panhandle, stinging the eyes of unfortunate travelers and causing them to lose their way. This was thought to be the fate of three young Mexican men who set out from Luxor on a burro, headed for El Wences, a town some hundred miles away to the south, to seek employment. They were mariachi singers, and they hoped to find work in one of the Mexican restaurants in El Wences.

They never reached their destination. In fact, they seemed to have just vanished in the mysterious darkness of *El ninja*.

It was while their friends were searching for the vanished trio that one of them revealed some new information. He said the young men had confided in him that they had a map showing the location of the lost Los Caballeros silver mine, and that they were going to try to find it.

The search continued in a different direction, but the three men were never seen again.

Sometimes, out of the dark cloud of *El ninja,* comes the sound of three-part mariachi singing, but in a mournful minor key. Some say this must be the lost singers, forever condemned to wander in the blackness of the mysterious cloud of dust, their punishment for daring to ignore the curse on the Los Caballeros mine.

Wilbarger

Near the town of Manor, not far from Austin, a strange event concerning two separate dreams has become a local legend. It happened in the early 1800s, when a man named Josiah Wilbarger moved to Texas from Missouri and built a small cabin in the uninhabited area. He was happy when an old friend, Reuben Hornsby, decided to come to Texas and settled in about two miles away from Wilbarger's place. Wilbarger visited often in his friend's home. Soon he was like a member of the family to Hornsby's wife, Sarah, and their eight children.

On a hunting trip, Wilbarger, Hornsby, and three other men were ambushed by a party of Indians. Two of the men were killed, and Wilbarger was wounded so badly that he couldn't escape. The others were certain he would die. As the survivors raced their horses through the woods, they chilled when they heard the blood-curdling war cries of the Indians as they moved in to scalp their victims.

Sarah Hornsby was very upset by the loss of their close friend, but her husband insisted there was nothing they could do. He felt lucky that he had escaped with his life.

The household finally settled down, but Sarah had a hard time getting to sleep. She slept for only a short while, and then sat up in bed, her eyes wide and staring. "Wilbarger is alive!" she cried.

This awakened her husband, and he tried to calm her. But she continued to insist that their friend was alive and in need of their help. "I saw him in a dream," she declared. "He is covered with blood and the Indians have scalped him, but he is alive and lying under a tree."

Had Sarah Hornsby been a different kind of woman, her husband might have ignored her dream. But she had proved herself time and time again to be of hardy pioneer stock. She had even fought off a party of Indians herself when her husband was away. Sarah was so certain that Wilbarger would die if they did not go to help him that she convinced her husband to find him. Another man from the hunting party was staying the night with them, and he went with Hornsby.

For fear the Indians might still be lurking about, the men decided not to leave until daybreak. Sarah furnished them with sheets to wrap the dead men in before they buried them. One sheet was to be used as a litter for poor Wilbarger who, she was sure, would be near death by the time they reached him.

The men rode to the spot where they had been attacked and found the bodies of their two friends.

Wilbarger was nowhere about, however. After they buried the dead men, they began to look for him. It was late afternoon when they spotted a figure with red skin lying under a tree. Thinking it to be an Indian, they drew their guns.

Before they could shoot, a faint voice called out, "Help me. I am Wilbarger."

The poor man had been stripped of all his clothing and scalped. His own blood, dried and caked, covered his body and gave him the reddish color. Wrapped in the sheet supplied by Sarah, Wilbarger, although weak and lapsing in and out of consciousness, was able to ride one of the horses back to the Hornsby cabin.

All Sarah Hornsby said was, "I knew you would find him alive."

After Wilbarger's wounds had been tended and he had rested for several days, he had a strange story of his own to tell. The shot which went through his neck paralyzed him and, mercifully, he felt no pain when the Indians scalped him. It was in his favor that he was unable to move and could not react to the horrible things he saw the Indians do. Because of this, the Indians thought he was dead, and left him alone after taking his scalp.

He was unconscious for a long time. When he came to, he realized that he was all alone, covered with dried blood and nothing more, and very thirsty. He dragged himself to a small spring that furnished water for the campsite, and he lay there in the water for a long time.

Night came and Wilbarger knew he was growing weaker, but he didn't know what to do. Then a remarkable thing happened. Suddenly, he saw quite clearly the figure of his sister, Margaret, who was still living in Missouri. They had been very close as children and had shared many happy times together. Wilbarger was certain now that he was about to die.

She spoke. "Stay here and rest, dear brother. Friends will be here soon to help you." Then she moved away in the direction of the Hornsby cabin. Wilbarger thought he must be delirious, but the figure of his sister was so clear and so comforting that he wanted to call out to her to stay with him.

It was not until many days later, when Wilbarger was on the way to recovery, that he received word from Missouri that his sister had died. The date of her death was the same day she appeared to him. And when Sarah and Wilbarger compared notes as to time, they found that Sarah had her dream soon after Margaret spoke to her wounded brother and assured him that help would come.

The Marfa Lights

The road leading to Marfa, Texas, is said to be one of the windiest and the coldest in winter of any to be found in the country. And the town itself is noted for its ghostly lights, which appear from time to time to mystify even the hardest-shelled doubters of anything spiritual.

At one time, there was an airport on Mitchell Flat on the outskirts of the town. The lights began to be seen there with such frequency and with sometimes tragic results, that the airport was shut down and the buildings abandoned.

Marfa residents who claim to have seen the ghost lights say that they do not remain in one spot, but play around and flicker like a campfire. Sometimes they seem to race along the edge of the mountain, resembling a prairie fire.

Since the first sightings, early in the 1900s, there have been efforts to pin down the lights and find out what causes them. Scientists and airplane pilots have attempted to get the lights cornered so that a logical explanation for their existence could

be offered. All these efforts, though, have come to nothing.

As is always the case in unexplainable phenomena, many legends have arisen about what the lights may be. Some of these go back to Indian days. One story arose after a party of Indians camped on the flat and were slaughtered by U.S. Army soldiers. It is said that the lights are ghosts of the Indians that have stolen lanterns from the settlers. They are waving the lanterns about in hopes of luring someone out to be killed in revenge.

Another Indian story says that a chief woke up one morning to find that all the others in his tribe had vanished. He wandered about the countryside, looking for his kinsmen, but never found any. When he died, his spirit continued the search, lighting the way with a lantern.

A later story says that a cowboy was caught out on the prairie during a terrible blizzard. He was certain he would freeze to death, since the snow was coming down like a blanket and he couldn't see which way to go. Suddenly, he saw the flashing of the Marfa lights, and somehow they communicated with him to follow them. He was led to a small cave, where he took shelter until the worst of the storm was over. When morning came, he found he was not far from his home.

Many of the older folk of the town declare the lights to be friendly. Farm animals are said to show no fear of them. Some people say they are the ghost of a rancher who once owned the land and was a good and God-fearing man. The lights shine brighter on his birthday, they say.

Others are equally certain that the lights are evil, and have caused the deaths of many investigators who went looking for them. There have been reports that men traveling in jeeps or other land vehicles were either burned to death or driven out of their minds. Their cars were reported to have been found melted down, as if by a white-hot fire.

It is also said that the lights have lured pilots to die against the rocky face of the Chinati Mountain cliffs. Some army men sent up in a helicopter to locate the lights disappeared when they landed in the spot where they thought them to be. Neither the men nor the aircraft were ever seen again.

One thing is certain: the appeal of the unknown is strong in the Marfa lights. Many of the legends about them have been around for a long time. Others have sprung from the active imaginations of local teenagers, who find the lights to have great appeal. The lights have also become a tourist attraction, with many folks traveling the long, lonely miles to Marfa each year in hopes of seeing them. And many do.

The Curse of
Old Chief Zolic

As a young man, Jim Bowie was not the heroic figure he later became. Before coming to Texas, Jim and a brother, Rezin, took part in all kinds of lawless ventures. Even after settling in the wide open Texas country, he didn't do much to change his ways. He was known as a heavy drinker, a brawler, a fighter of duels, and a man always on the lookout for ways to make money.

He had not been in Texas long before he met and fell in love with Ursulita, the beautiful daughter of the vice-governor of the territory. Jim had already become a Mexican citizen. And now, to increase his chances with the young lady, he converted to the Catholic faith.

It was about this time that rumors of a rich silver mine owned by the Lipan Indians in San Saba reached Jim's ears. He was told that these Indians often came to San Antonio with nuggets of pure silver to trade for food and weapons.

Since Jim knew he could not ask Ursulita to marry him unless he was a man of means, he began

to ask around about the Lipans. He arranged to
meet their chief, an old warrior by the name of Zolic.
Jim made a point to impress him with his manliness
and his skill with the Bowie knife. Soon the two men
were friends, and old Zolic invited Jim to spend some
time with his tribe in San Saba. Jim was delighted
to accept. He became a great favorite with the
braves and was almost like a son to the old chief.
They called him *Cuchilla Grande,* which means "Big
Knife."

After living with the Indians for almost a year,
Jim was accepted into the tribe. He was told the se-
crets of the Lipans. Although some of the young
braves were against it, Chief Zolic even told him the
location of the silver mine.

Jim was elated. As soon as he could manage it, he slipped away and hurried back to San Antonio to tell what he knew to his brother. Rezin began at once to organize a band of men to plunder the mine while Jim renewed his courtship of Ursulita. After all, he would soon be a wealthy man and could offer her all the luxuries she required.

They were married in 1831, and Jim felt he was the luckiest man in the world. Then bad news came. Old Chief Zolic had died, and now the chief of the tribe was a husky brave by the name of Tres Manos. The new chief hated Jim because Zolic's daughter had shown great interest in the white man, and may have married him in a tribal rite. Historians are vague on that point. At any rate, Tres Manos wanted the Indian princess for his own, and was furious that she preferred Jim.

Word was sent to Jim by the new chief that he was no longer welcome in the Lipan camp. And Jim was told that Chief Zolic had placed an ancient curse on him for his treachery after the Lipan people had trusted him. He was cursed to never be able to find the silver mine again. Jim knew now that they would have to take the mine away from the Indians by force.

With Rezin and the band of fighters he had organized, Jim set out. They met the Lipans, some two hundred strong, on the banks of Calf Creek. A fierce battle ensued. Somehow, Jim's small band managed to beat off several attacks by the larger force in one of the fiercest Indian battles in Texas history. Finally, the wounded Tres Manos limped away into the woods, followed by his braves. He was never seen again, and may have died of his wounds.

After camping several days to recover from the battle, Jim and his men went in search of the mine. They could not locate it. Two more times, Jim led expeditions to San Saba to try to find the spot marked on the map given him by the old chief. But the closer they came, the more confused and disoriented Jim seemed to become. Some say this was because of Chief Zolic's curse.

Even more misfortune was to befall him. Years after his unsuccessful attempts to find silver, his wife Ursulita and their small children, a son and a daughter, died of a strange plague that swept into Texas from Louisiana. Heartbroken, Jim tried to lose himself in the fight for Texas' independence from Mexico. Eventually he found himself under siege in the Alamo with other brave men.

While trying to place a small cannon on the ramparts to fight off the Mexican attack that was soon to come, Jim lost his balance and took a bad fall. Some ribs were broken, and one punctured his lung. Without proper medical attention, Jim's condition quickly grew serious. When the final attack came, he was in great pain and hot with fever. His heroic death, fighting with his Bowie knife from his cot, is a matter of historic record.

The San Saba silver mines have never been found. Whether the old chief was confused in the directions he gave to his adopted son, or whether he did, indeed, place a curse on Jim for betraying him, will never be known.

The Phantom Spaceship

In the early April dawn in 1897, a cigar-shaped, brightly-lit airship circled the square of the little town of Aurora in Wise County. Then it crashed and exploded. Or so the story goes.

There had been earlier sightings of this strange craft. Persons in several Midwestern states had reported seeing it, and earlier in the month, the strange sight had been reported by citizens of Denton, Weatherford, and Corsicana. No official action had been taken, however, because at that time the airplane had yet to be invented. The only method for humans to become airborne was the hot air balloon.

Those who were brave enough to go out to the site where the ship had crashed found that the pilot was dead. Supposedly, papers on his body identified him as coming from the planet Mars.

Believing that even a creature from another planet deserved a decent burial, several local citizens held a funeral. The body was interred, and a small stone was placed to mark the location of the

34

grave. After a brief flurry of interest and an article in the local paper, the incident seemed to be forgotten.

Years passed. In 1973, rumors of UFOs were rampant, and someone remembered the Aurora spaceship. It was reported to the UFO Bureau, which sent a team of experts to Texas to investigate.

They found that there were, indeed, fragments of metal at the crash site that could not be identified as any known to us. They learned that after the crash, nothing would ever grow on the land immediately surrounding it. A search for the grave was unsuccessful. It seemed to have disappeared.

All eyewitnesses to the fly-over of the spaceship and its crash nearby were dead, but some folks living in the area repeated stories that had been told them by parents and grandparents. Finally, the investigators had to leave, admitting that they could come to no definite conclusion.

Did it really happen or not? Did an alien being crash his spaceship on a farm near Aurora more than a hundred years ago? Those who were told about it as children from family members who claimed to have actually seen the spaceship declare it had to be true. Investigators from the UFO Bureau are more guarded, saying it *could* have happened.

So, it seems to be left up to the individual to decide. To quote a familiar phrase coined by Ripley, believe it or not!

Indian Emily

Inside Fort Davis in far West Texas, there stands a historical marker, erected by the state of Texas during the centennial year of 1936. It reads:

Here lies Indian Emily
An Apache girl
Whose love for a
Young Officer Induced Her
To Give Warning Of
An Indian Attack
Mistaken For An Enemy
She Was Shot By A Sentry
But Saved The Garrison
From Massacre

Before this marker, the grave of Indian Emily was covered by a board which said simply: Indian Squaw Killed By Accident.

The Apache maiden whose body lies in the grave was named Indian Emily by folktellers of the region, and many different stories are told of how she came to be buried inside a U.S. Army fortress.

In 1867, Fort Davis, in the heart of Apache country, was often attacked by hostile braves. The

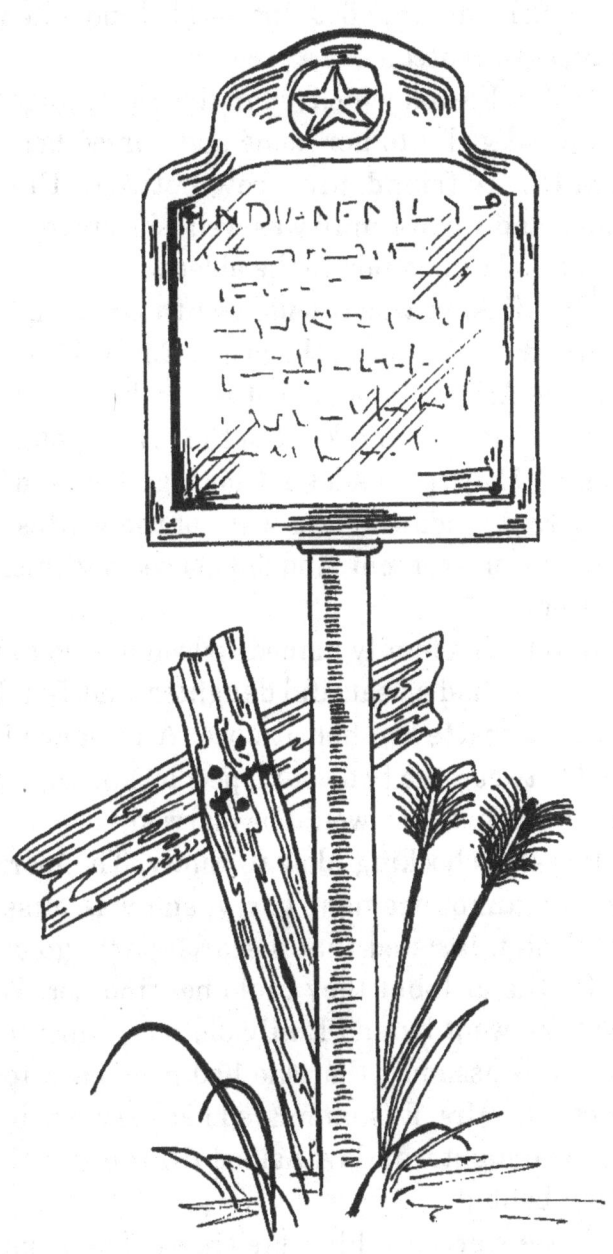

story is told that during one such skirmish, a young Indian girl was wounded and left behind when the attackers retreated.

A Mrs. Easton who lived in the community took the injured girl into her home and nursed her back to health. A friendship grew between the two women, and when Emily was well, she stayed on as servant and companion to the older woman.

Mrs. Easton was a widow with one son, Tom, who was a lieutenant in the army. Emily fell in love with him. Although he did not return her affections, Tom was friendly and kind to the lovely young Indian girl. They spent a lot of time together, and Tom helped Emily adapt to the ways of the whites. She was happy and content, and did not seem to miss her own people.

And then a family named Nelson moved to Fort Davis. They had a beautiful daughter, and Tom Easton was attracted to her at once. A romance blossomed between the two young people, and soon they announced that they would be married.

It was a shocking blow to Emily. The morning after the announcement party, she was missing. Mrs. Easton insisted that a search party go out to look for the girl, but they could not find her. When some time went by and Emily did not return to the fort, it was assumed that she had gone back to her own people. Mrs. Easton missed her very much, but her new daughter-in-law helped fill the gap Emily had left behind.

These were troublesome times. The Apaches

were growing bolder, and there were more and more raids on outlying settlements. The soldiers assigned to Fort Davis were kept busy. And at times, the fort itself was left poorly manned when help was needed elsewhere. Everyone was on edge, and the least unexpected movement from outside the barricades made the sentries jumpy.

One night, a lone soldier on guard heard running footsteps approaching the fort. He called out, "Halt!" When the footsteps did not stop, but came nearer, the soldier took aim at a dim, running figure and fired. A woman screamed, and then there was silence.

The soldier hurried forward to see who had been hit, and found it to be the Indian girl, Emily. Mrs. Easton was called, and she knelt beside her dying friend, gathering her into her arms.

"I hear my people talk — many warriors," the girl gasped. "Coming here — soon. Tell Tom — " And then she died.

The Indians did come, but Emily's warning had given the time needed to arm the fort, and the savage warriors were driven back. Emily was buried some distance from the main part of the fort, and for a time, Mrs. Easton tended her grave. When Tom was transferred and the Eastons moved away, Indian Emily seemed to be forgotten.

But strange things began to happen. On still nights, when the "Comanche Moon" was high, the anguished scream of a woman would split the night air. Sometimes there would be light, running footsteps, and often, from the direction of Emily's grave, could be heard the sound of soft, heartbroken sobbing.

The more practical-minded of the area declared the screams to be merely those of a panther, many of which roamed the mountains nearby. The footsteps and the weeping were only the sounds of the constant West Texas winds, stirring the tall grass and brush that surrounded Emily's grave.

Interest was renewed in the story of Emily, however, and the narrow, overgrown trail that led to the grave was graded and made more passable by the army. Curious people wanted to see where the brave Indian maiden lay. Often they stayed after dark, in hopes of hearing the ghostly sounds. The grave became enough of a tourist attraction in later years to cause the state to build a historical marker to point to Indian Emily's final resting place.

The Ghost of Mustang Gray

Mabry Gray was one bad *hombre*. He just showed up on the streets of Victoria one day, back in the early 1800s, and began to make a name for himself as a really bad man.

He set up his headquarters down near where the Guadalupe and San Antonio rivers meet, and gathered a gang of cutthroats around him to terrorize that part of Texas. They rustled cattle, stole horses, smuggled contraband, did just about everything that was against the law, and murdered anyone who tried to stand in their way.

Blond and blue-eyed, Mabry claimed he came to Texas to escape hanging for murdering his sweetheart's brother. Soon he acquired the nickname "Mustang," and no one ever called him Mabry after that.

No crime was too horrible or heartless for Mustang and his gang. They preyed on ranchers and townspeople alike, and cared for no one but themselves.

Finally, they went too far. They made friends

with some tradesmen from Mexico who had come to Victoria in good faith to buy tobacco and other goods in exchange for silver and leather goods from their country. As the Mexicans were camping at Goliad on the return trip home, Mustang and his men fell on them and slaughtered them with no mercy. Someone offered a reward for the capture of the murderers, but Mustang slipped away and headed west for a time.

He didn't change his ways, however. News came back that he was still leaving a bloody trail everywhere he went. He killed anyone who crossed him in any way, and a few who were in the wrong place and unlucky that Mustang happened to be there too.

What finally did Mustang in was not a bullet from a lawman's gun nor the stab of a knife from someone seeking revenge. He was a heavy drinker, and one night he downed a whole bottle of bad whiskey. He passed out and died on the floor of a saloon.

Mustang was buried near his old hideout on the banks of the San Antonio River, but no marker was placed on the grave. In time, it was whispered that he was not really there, but that his spirit still haunted the streets and bars of old Victoria.

So convincing were the stories about seeing Mustang's ghost that even the toughest old cowboys glanced over their shoulders when they had to be out alone on dark and windy nights. In their hearts, they were certain that Mustang was just too mean to stay dead.

When one of the local ranchowners who had

been a bitter enemy of the outlaw died, several of his cowboys sat up with his body the night before the funeral, according to the custom of the day. They were nervous that this might be a time when the spirit of Mustang would choose to appear.

Shortly after midnight, something white crashed through the window, clattered across the floor, and was out the door in an instant.

"Mustang's ghost!" the cowboys shrieked, scattering in all directions.

At dawn, they ventured out of their hiding places to find an old white billy goat, tangled up in the lace curtain that had been in the window, calmly eating grass in the yard. They laughed and pretended they had been the victims of a practical joke. But in their hearts, they were never really sure.

The Eerie House Call

The young doctor and his wife had planned to spend a quiet evening at home. They were chatting happily in front of the fireplace, enjoying after-dinner coffee, when someone pulled the bell at the front door.

"Oh, no," sighed the young wife, knowing this meant her husband would probably have to leave.

The doctor patted her hand and got up to see who was, by this time, pounding frantically on the door. Peering through the glass, he saw a Spanish gentleman with long, wavy hair and a wide, drooping mustache. The man was dressed in the ruffled shirt, tight silk pants, and high boots of a style many years past. Puzzled, the doctor opened the door.

"*Señor* Doctor," the man said, in obvious distress. "Please to come with me at once. There has been an accident. My daughter —"

The doctor told the man to wait while he hitched up his horse and buggy. On a whim, he asked his wife to accompany him. It was a clear, cool November night, and, after all, they had planned an evening together.

The Spaniard, mounted now on his horse, had been waiting impatiently by the hitching post. He set off at once down the street leading out of the city of San Antonio.

"It's probably not too serious," the doctor said to his wife as they rode along. "His daughter has been hurt. That's all I know."

The young wife smiled. "Were they at a costume ball?" she asked. "That man looks like a picture in a history book."

It was certainly not to a ball that they were being led. The streets were becoming narrower and the houses smaller and farther apart. As they left the lights of the town behind, the night seemed to become even darker. The doctor began to feel uneasy as the rider turned into a narrow lane shadowed by great trees on either side.

Suddenly, they were in the courtyard of a big house, square and tall with great white columns stretching up into the gloom. The rider dismounted and ran back to the buggy.

"Come!" he cried, harshly.

"Shall my wife accompany us?" the doctor asked. "Perhaps she could be of help."

"No! Leave her here. She will be safe."

The doctor followed the Spaniard into a wide hall, and then into a small, dimly-lit room to the right. Lying on a fancy embroidered sofa was a young woman. She was a beautiful Spanish girl with long dark hair, pale white skin, and large black eyes, now filled with fear and pain. One shoulder of the lovely, old-fashioned satin gown she wore was stained with blood.

Speaking reassuring words, the doctor bent over the girl, tore apart the sleeve, and inspected the wound. The man stood silently in the shadows.

"It's nothing serious," the doctor said. "Looks as if she may have been grazed by a bullet."

He straightened, and it was then he noticed the bloodstains on the floor, a large pool at the end of the sofa, and then a trail of crimson drops leading to some French doors on the other side of the room.

"Would you care to tell me what happened here?" the doctor asked.

"No!" The word came sharply from the darkness. "Please to tend to her, that is all. I will pay."

The doctor turned back to the girl and dressed her wound. She did not flinch, but he could feel her large, dark eyes staring at him, pleading with him. He realized she was in more than physical pain, but didn't know what he could do to help.

When he was finished, he closed his bag, stood, and said to the man, "Bring her by my house tomorrow so that I can dress her wound properly. There could be danger of infection."

He walked past the man and felt coins being pressed into his hand. Then he was outside. His wife clutched at him in fear as he stepped up into the buggy.

"Let's get out of here," she whispered. "There's

46

something out there under the trees making strange, moaning sounds. I'm frightened."

"Ah, it's only the wind," he reassured her, knowing the night to be still, without even a breeze. He whipped up his horse into a gallop. When once again they had reached the safety of lighted streets, he told his wife about the young girl and the blood-stained floor.

"We must report it to the police," she said.

"Perhaps I can learn more when I see the girl to-morrow," the doctor replied. "She's coming to have her wound dressed."

The girl did not come the next day, nor the next. On the third day, the doctor went to the police and reported what he had seen. A deputy, an old man, got up from his desk.

"Let me go with him," he said to the other officers. "I know the way."

Again the doctor left the city, this time with the old deputy by his side. Again he turned into the narrow lane, almost as gloomy by day as by night. When they came to the clearing where the big square house had stood, the doctor gasped in shock. Before him was a crumbling ruin, with flaking paint and broken windows. The roof sagged, and part of one column was gone.

He leaped out of the buggy and ran into the house. In the room where the girl had been were the tattered remains of a once-fine sofa, ravaged by time and wild animals. Everything was covered by a thick layer of dust, and there were no bloodstains on the floor.

"I know how you feel." The voice of the deputy who had followed him into the house startled the young doctor. "It happened to me once too."

The doctor frowned. "I don't understand. Just two nights ago —"

"I know," the deputy interrupted. "You were brought here by a fine looking aristocratic Spanish gentleman to help his daughter."

The doctor nodded, and the deputy went on. "So was I — a much younger man then and quite taken with the beautiful girl I found here. But the blood-stains on the floor bothered me, and I told them to come to the police station the next day to fill out a report. They never did."

The old deputy sighed. "When I came back out the next day, this is what I found. I was as disturbed as you, and I started asking questions, trying to make some sense out of it. I was finally told the story by an old, old man who has lived in San Antonio all his life.

"When the city was young, this was a fine house owned by a rich Spanish lady. She had a beautiful niece who had the bad luck to fall in love with a common foot soldier stationed here. The girl's father forbade her to see the man she loved, but the aunt let them meet here in her home when she was traveling abroad.

"One night, the father followed them and shot the young soldier. The girl tried to shield her lover and was wounded, and the soldier escaped into the woods."

The old voice faltered. "The day I came back, I saw him — all covered with blood — out there in the woods. When I went to help him, no one was there."

"This is unbelievable," the young doctor cried. "You say this happened a long time ago?"

"More than a hundred years. Many people have seen the ghosts — just as you and I. But no one talks about it."

"What happened to the girl and her father?"

"I suppose they left San Antonio. The body of the soldier was never found, and the aunt refused to come back to the house. It was left to become — this." He waved his arm about the deserted mansion.

In a few years after the doctor's house call, even that was gone, washed away in a flood. And so, the restless ghosts are seen no more.

The Man with the Yellow-Green Eyes

In the days following the Civil War, a tall, dark man with strange, yellow-green eyes bought and cleared some land in the piney woods of East Texas. The man planted corn on the cleared land and sold timber, and became quite wealthy. He lived alone in a gloomy, two-storied house in the middle of his fields. Since he said his name was Cole, the place came to be known as Cole's Plantation.

It was not hard for Cole to find help. Many families were moving south to Texas to escape the hard times up north after the war. They often stopped at Cole's, attracted by the generous wages he offered the men to help harvest his crops and cut his timber.

Soon, however, chilling rumors began to spread about Cole and his plantation. Some of the men who hired on as laborers, especially single ex-soldiers who were working their way back to their homes, were never seen again. They seemed to disappear just before their first payday. The other men may have wondered, but they dared not question Cole about anything. The way he stared at whoever he

was talking to with his slanted, yellow-green eyes made any questions remain unasked.

A family named Smith from Tennessee stopped for a time at Cole's place, and the father hired on as a laborer to earn enough money to get them farther south. They moved into one of the small shacks provided by Cole for his workers. After a day or two, Smith told his wife they were moving on after his first payday.

"That man gives me the creeps," Smith said. "I started to take a short-cut through that cornfield out back of his house today, and he yelled at me like I was tryin' to steal something. One of the men told me no one goes in that cornfield."

Payday finally came. Smith planned to stop by the big house after his day's work to get his money, and then they were moving on. The wagon was packed, and Mrs. Smith and six-year-old Amy sat in the small cabin, waiting for Smith's return.

The day grew late, and a chilly rain began to fall. Mrs. Smith added more logs to the fire, afraid now they would have to wait until morning to begin their journey.

Darkness fell. Mrs. Smith began to worry. Suddenly, there came a terrible howling sound on the porch, like the cry of the big wildcats in the mountains of Tennessee.

"Mama!" said the little girl. "I'm scared!"

"It's only an old tomcat," the mother replied. "I'll scare him off."

But before she could move, the door blew open, and a huge black cat walked in. Its yellow-green eyes gleamed in the light from the fire, and its tail lashed from side to side.

Mrs. Smith pushed her daughter behind her and picked up a stick of firewood. "Get out of here!" she yelled, brandishing the weapon. "Scat! Scat!"

The great cat stood its ground, staring at the woman with its slanted eyes. Although rain was pounding on the roof of the cabin, she noticed that the fur of the cat was dry, and that it left no wet tracks on the floor. After a long moment, it turned and stalked out the door. Mrs. Smith sprang to shut and lock the door, and then she propped a heavy chair against it.

"Mama," the little girl said softly, huddling close to her mother's skirts, "that cat had eyes just like — like Mr. Cole's."

Soon Smith returned, tired, wet, and angry. "That devil Cole made us stand out in the rain to get our pay, and then he never showed up."

From just outside the door, the cat yowled again. In whispers, Mrs. Smith told her husband what had happened. He walked to the mantel, took down his shotgun, and went to the door.

"You and Amy stay inside," he said to his wife. "I'll take care of it." Then he opened the door and stepped out into the rain. The cat wailed again, this time from the edge of the yard. Smith went after it, his gun ready.

Mrs. Smith and her daughter waited anxiously. When her husband returned to them some time later, he was white-faced and trembling.

"Get your things into the wagon," he ordered. "We're leaving this place right now."

Once they were miles away from Cole's Plantation, Smith told his wife what had happened to him. He followed the large black cat in the dark and rain, trying to get close enough for a good shot. The creature kept howling as if taunting him to come on.

At last, Smith realized they were at the edge of the forbidden cornfield. The cat stopped and turned to look at his pursuer with its slanted, yellow-green eyes. As Smith raised the gun to his shoulder to fire, the cat disappeared.

Thinking it had run into the cornfield, Smith

followed down a row, determined to find the creature. Suddenly, he stumbled over a mound of earth and fell to his knees. He looked around and saw that there were other mounds, among the rows of corn. Graves! He was certain of it.

Horrified, he struggled to his feet and turned to run away. And then in the darkness, just a step or two ahead, he saw a yawning black hole, recently dug. It was waiting, he knew now, for him. Had he not fallen when he did, he would have been just another laborer who vanished from the earth after working a few days for the man with the yellow-green eyes.

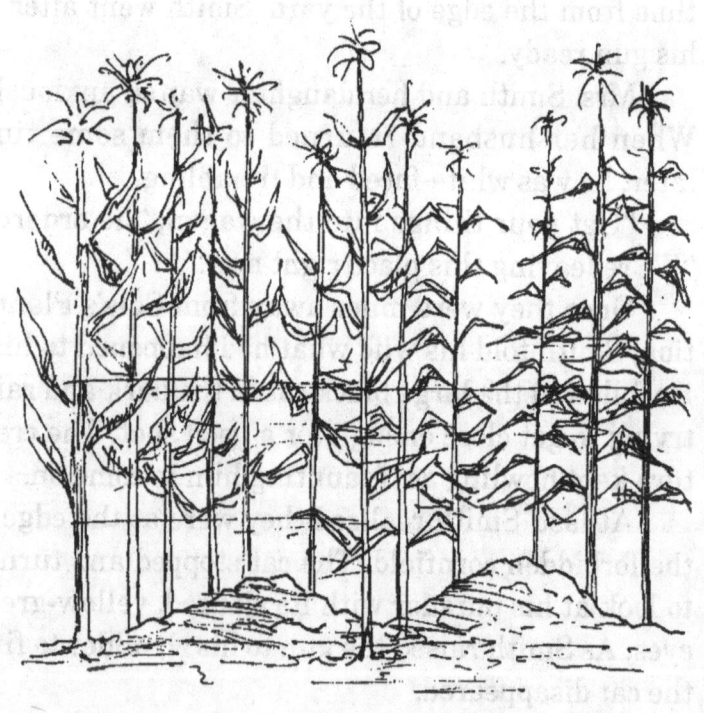

The Ghostly Pianist

In the Victorian days, the beautiful mansion called Ashton Villa, on Broadway in Galveston, was the scene of many lavish balls and formal recitals. It was the home of wealthy financier John M. Brown and his family.

The darling of the Brown clan, and of Galveston society as well, was the youngest daughter, Rebecca. Lively and full of fun, she was known to everyone as Miss Bettie. Her favorite thing to do was to sit down at the big piano in the Gold Room of the mansion and entertain anyone who might be there with popular tunes of the day.

As she got older, Miss Bettie became a "free spirit," pushing aside the many rules proper young ladies of that time were supposed to follow. She shocked family and friends by smoking in public, traveling alone, and entertaining many sweethearts.

She had some talent as an artist, and she used this as an excuse to go to Europe, supposedly to study under the great masters. Her father disapproved, but she went anyway. Although she did take some art lessons, she spent most of her time partying through the continent with royalty and the social elite.

Her way of life was an embarrassment to her family. Finally, her father ordered her to return home. When she refused, he disowned her, and forbade her to ever enter Ashton Villa again.

The two were never reunited. John Brown died suddenly, some said of a broken heart. Miss Bettie remained in Europe until she, too, died. She was alone, having never married.

Ashton Villa is now a museum, and in the Gold Room hang two paintings signed by Miss Bettie and sent to her family. Their places of honor on the walls of Miss Bettie's favorite room would suggest that her father forgave her at last.

And there are those who say that Miss Bettie has returned to her home as well. A caretaker who lived in a small cottage near the mansion was awakened one night by the sound of piano music coming from the Villa. It was after midnight, and he feared that vandals might have somehow entered the house. He let himself in and slipped quietly down the wide hall.

The music was coming from the Gold Room. The caretaker eased the door open, expecting to confront a drunken mischief-maker. Instead, his startled eyes saw a woman in Victorian garb seated at the piano. She was almost transparent and there was a shimmering aura about her.

Frightened, he flooded the room with light, and instantly, both woman and music were gone. Somehow he knew that he had seen Miss Bettie, whose name was mentioned often by people who visited the museum.

From then on, when the caretaker heard the haunting music late at night, he stayed in his cottage. He had no wish to disturb Miss Bettie, who had come home at last to play on her beloved piano in her favorite room.

The Lonely Watchman

He was first seen in 1850 by a young boy. The tall, erect Indian chief stood motionless on top of a hill outside the small Central Texas town of Tehuacana. This was unusual because there had been no Indians in that part of Texas for many years. What was more unusual was that one moment he was there, his dark eyes staring westward as if looking for someone, and the next moment he was gone, vanished into thin air.

Others would see him. He was identified as a chief of the vanquished Tawakoni tribe, victim of a terrible massacre in the early 1800s. The friendly, peaceable Tawakoni were wiped out by a fierce Indian tribe that swooped down upon them one day. The warriors caught them by surprise, killed as many as they could, and destroyed the village. A few escaped, among them the chief's small son. The father died in the battle.

The young boy was carefully guarded by the few survivors. He would be their chief one day and would gather the tattered remnants of the Tawakoni into a tribe once more.

It didn't happen. The boy grew up, made friends with the whites, and became an Indian scout for the United States cavalry. Proud of his heritage, he took the name Tawakoni Jim, and served his adopted people bravely and well.

The people of Tehuacana who know about the lonely figure on the hill say it is the ghost of the old Tawakoni chief, looking out over the plains and valleys of Central Texas for the sight of his beloved son. They say he cannot rest because he believes the surprise raid that caught his people off-guard was his fault.

After Tawakoni Jim died at the age of ninety, it was thought that the sightings of the old chief would end as well. But he still appears, briefly, if you are lucky enough to see him — a tall, motionless, solitary figure, the broken-hearted ghost of a dream that never came to be.

The Lady
in the Theater

The trendy Olla Podrida Mall in north Dallas is a popular shopping place for persons looking for handcrafted and unusual gift items. For a time a dinner theater, the Gaslight Playhouse, was located in one wing of the mall.

Soon after the theater opened, the actors began to notice a woman dressed in a clothing style that was popular around the turn of the century. She sat in the back row during rehearsals. When anyone spoke to her or walked down the aisle toward her, she disappeared.

This was disturbing to the theater people at first. But as time went on and the woman did nothing threatening, they jokingly referred to her as their "resident ghost" and left her alone. She was not there every night, and no one saw her come or go. They would look to the back of the theater and on occasion, she would be there, quiet and motionless.

Then they began to experience cold spots at various places in the theater, and sometimes they saw a hazy, misty light hanging over the seats. One night, when the manager was closing up and everyone else had gone, there came a blinding flash of blue light and a loud ringing sound. It lasted for only a moment, but the frightened man hurried out, locking the door behind him. The next day, everything appeared to be normal.

Whether or not the "resident ghost" had anything to do with it, the theater went out of business. Since that time, nothing more has been seen of the ghostly figure. Apparently, she was interested only in the theater and not the rest of the mall.